Andy Griffiths is one of Australia's funniest and most successful authors. He has won several awards and his books are bestsellers the world over. He lives in Melbourne with his wife and two daughters.

Terry Denton is a Melbourne writer and illustrator of children's books who has collaborated with Andy Griffiths on ten books. He loves the challenge of finding new and exciting ways of entertaining their readers.

Also by Andy Griffiths and Terry Denton

*The Cat on the Mat Is Flat*

*What Bumosaur Is That?*

The JUST books:

*Just Annoying!*
*Just Crazy!*
*Just Disgusting!*
*Just Kidding!*
*Just Stupid!*

'Just hilarious, screwball, ridiculous and very, very funny'
*Bookseller*

Also by Andy Griffiths, for older readers

The BUM books:

*The Day My Bum Went Psycho*
'Surreal . . . disgusting lavatorial jokes drove me crazy but
made my kids laugh like a drain' *Independent on Sunday*

*Zombie Bums from Uranus*
'No ifs or butts – this book will crack you up!'
*Poos of the World*

*Bumageddon . . . The Final Pongflict*
'Andy Griffiths's sense of the stupid and subversive
goes up to the top of the hill and down the other side
in *Bumageddon*' *Sunday Morning Post*

# ANDY GRIFFITHS & TERRY DENTON

# THE BIG FAT COW THAT GOES KAPOW!

MACMILLAN CHILDREN'S BOOKS

First published 2008 in Pan by Pan Macmillan Australia Pty Ltd

First published in the UK 2009 by Macmillan Children's Books
a division of Macmillan Publishers Limited
20 New Wharf Road, London N1 9RR
Basingstoke and Oxford
Associated companies throughout the world
www.panmacmillan.com

ISBN 978-0-330-45637-1

1 3 5 7 9 8 6 4 2

A CIP catalogue record for this book is available from the British Library.

Printed and bound in the UK by CPI Mackays, Chatham ME5 8TD

# Contents

# BIG FAT COWS

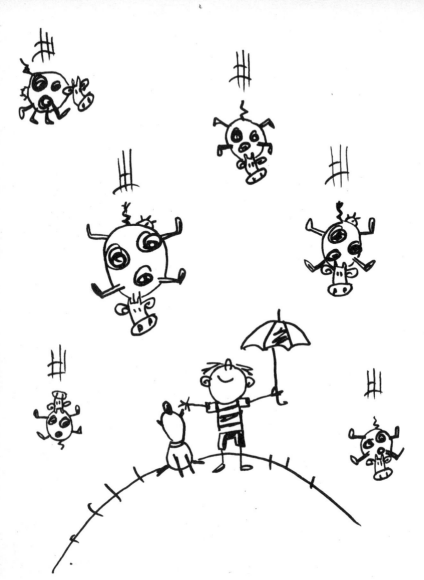

It's raining
big fat cows
today.

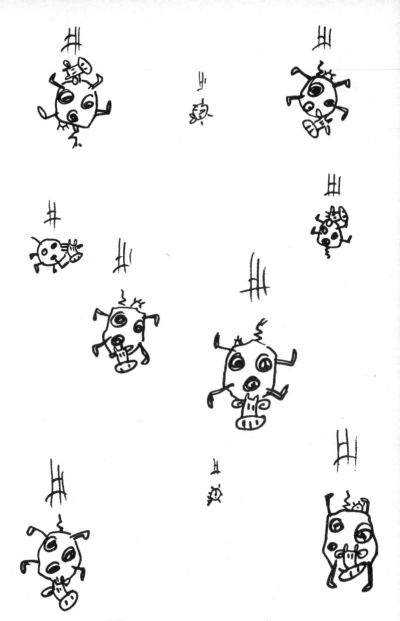

How many cows?
It's hard to say.

A big cow here.

A fat cow there.

Big fat cows are

EVERY

# WHERE!

Cows underwater.

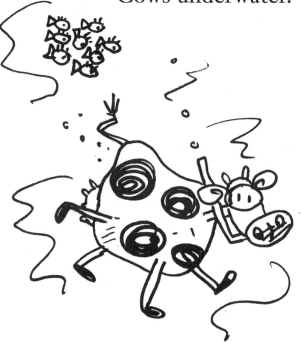

Cows in space.

Big fat cows
all over the place!

10

Cows in boats.

Cows in suits.

Big fat cows
in cowboy boots!

This one is a
mixed-up cow.
It flaps its wings
and says miaow!

Oh no – watch out!
Don't look now!

This one is an

EXPLODING cow . . .

# NOEL THE MOLE

Here is a hole.

A deep,
dark
hole.

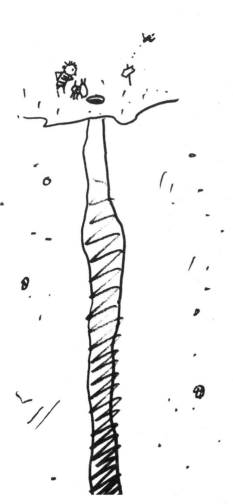

In this hole
lives a mole
called Noel.

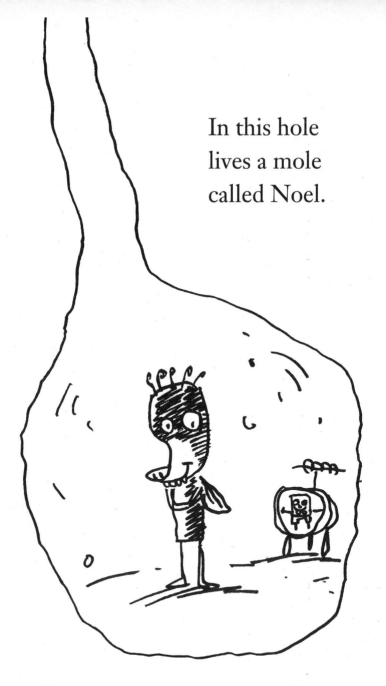

He eats
black coal.

He plays
rock and roll.

27

And
that's
the
whole
story
of
the
mole
called
Noel –
he's a
hole-dwelling,
coal-eating
rock-and-roll
mole!

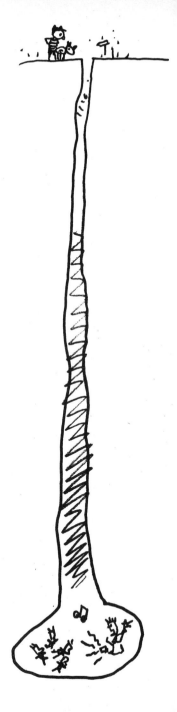

# KLAUS THE MOUSE

This
is
Klaus.

Klaus
is a
mouse.

Klaus
the
mouse
has
a
very
small
house.

A
very,
very,
very,
very,
very

small
house.

But Klaus
the mouse
hates his
small house . . .

because
Klaus
is
a

# VERY,

# VERY,

# VERY

# BI

mouse!

# WILLY THE WORM

This is Willy.
Willy the worm.

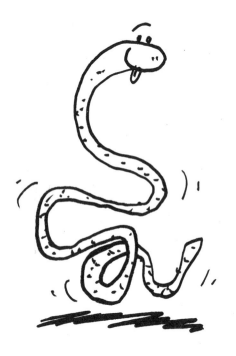

He goes to
squirm school
to learn how
to squirm.

But Willy the worm
is a very bad learner.

He's wiggly
on the
straight,

and a
terrible
turner!

Willy never pays attention,
and he mucks around a lot.

He always ends up
in a great big knot!

# KEITH, ED AND DAISY

Here is a man
called Three-coat Keith.
He wears one coat on top
and two underneath.

Keith has a brother
called Five-hat Ed.

He wears five hats
on top of his head.

And this
is their sister,
One-dress Daisy.

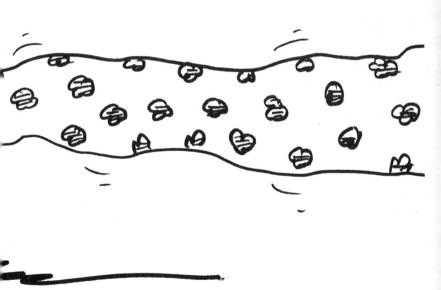

She shares her dress
with her best friend, Maisie.

# LUMPY-HEAD

# FRED

Have you heard
about the boy called
Lumpy-head Fred?

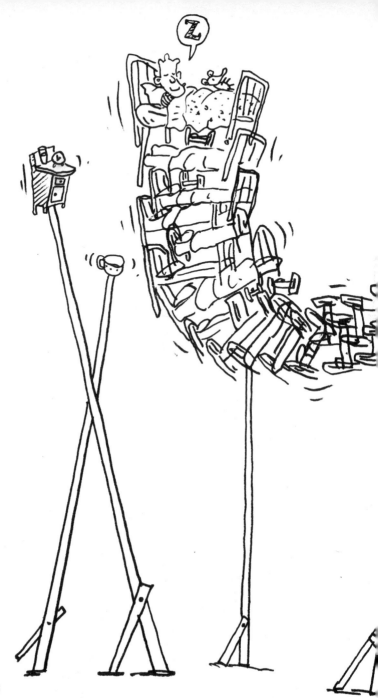

He sleeps
at the top
of a
hundred-decker
bed!

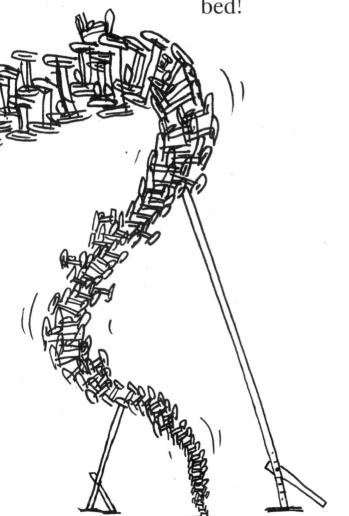

But
poor
old
Fred
always
falls
out of
bed.

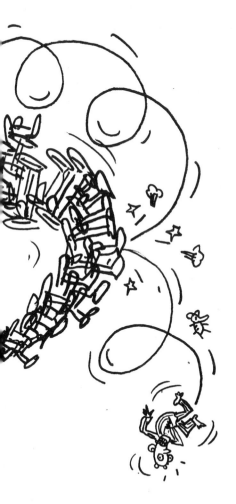

Which
is why
he has
such a
lumpy
bumpy
head.

# BRAVE DAVE

This is Dave,
who, during the day,
is

# REALLY,

# REALLY,

# REALLY

# BRAVE!

But during the night,
when there's no light,
Dave is NOT brave.
He takes fright.

Each noise he hears
increases his fears.

Every BUMP,

every THUMP

makes his
poor heart
# JUMP!

He sucks
his thumb.

He calls
for his
mum.

He can't wait
for the
morning
to come.

So if you need
a brave job done,
call Dave in the day . . .

but at night
call his mum.

# RUTH'S SUPER SCOOTER

Here comes Ruth.
Ruth rides a scooter.
Ruth rides a scooter
with a super-loud hooter.

75

# With a super-hoot here . . .

and a super-hoot there.

Here a hoot.

There a hoot.

# Everywhere
# a super-hoot!

We think Ruth
would be a LOT cuter
if she'd only stop blowing
her super-loud hooter.

# MIKE'S BIKE

Here comes Mike.
Mike rides a bike.

Mike rides a bike
with a . . .

ve

ry

big

spike!

We don't like Mike
or his big spiky bike.

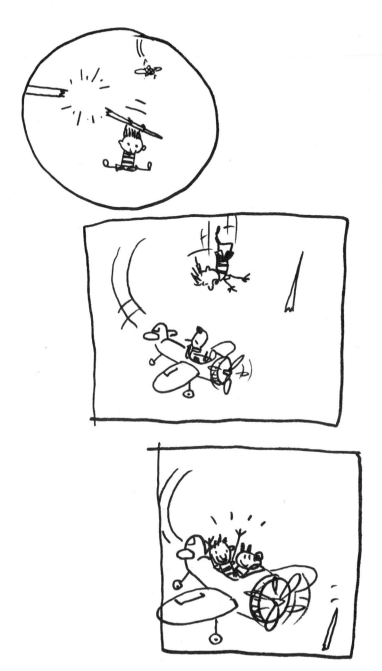

Let's go somewhere
a little less Mikey!

Let's go somewhere
a little less spiky!

# SOMEWHERE LESS SPIKY

Here is a town
that is really incredible.
You can eat what you like
because
everything is edible.

Here is a sea
where you
can breathe
underwater.

You can stay
underwater
for an hour
AND a quarter.

Here is
a planet
where people
can fly.

And the clouds
are like
trampolines
up in the sky.

And here is a land
with big fat
rain.

It's raining
big fat cows
again!

A big cow here.

A fat cow there.

Big fat cows are

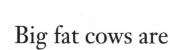

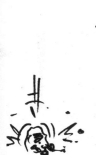

EVERY

# WHERE!

Oh no – watch out!
Don't look now!
Here comes that
EXPLODING cow . . .

# FoUR

# THREE

# Two

# TURN OVER FOR A
# GIGGLE-PACKED PREVIEW OF

## ANDY GRIFFITHS & TERRY DENTON

# OUT NOW!

The cat sat.

The cat sat on the mat.

The cat sat on the mat
and as it sat
it saw a rat.

The cat jumped up
and chased
the rat

around
and around
and around
the mat.

The rat did not like
being chased by the cat,
and after three laps
around the mat

the rat said,
'That's enough of that!'
And it went
and got . . .

# a baseball bat.

# A selected list of titles available from Macmillan Children's Books

The prices shown below are correct at the time of going to press. However, Macmillan Publishers reserves the right to show new retail prices on covers, which may differ from those previously advertised.

## Andy Griffiths & Terry Denton

| | | |
|---|---|---|
| The Cat on the Mat Is Flat | 978-0-330-45636-4 | £4.99 |
| What Bumosaur Is That? | 978-0-330-44752-2 | £4.99 |
| Just Annoying! | 978-0-330-39729-2 | £4.99 |
| Just Crazy! | 978-0-330-39727-8 | £4.99 |
| Just Disgusting! | 978-0-330-41592-7 | £4.99 |
| Just Kidding! | 978-0-330-39728-5 | £4.99 |
| Just Stupid! | 978-0-330-39726-1 | £4.99 |

## Andy Griffiths

| | | |
|---|---|---|
| The Day My Bum Went Psycho | 978-0-330-40089-3 | £4.99 |
| Zombie Bums from Uranus | 978-0-330-43680-9 | £4.99 |
| Bumageddon ... The Final Pongflict | 978-0-330-43370-9 | £4.99 |

All Pan Macmillan titles can be ordered from our website, www.panmacmillan.com, or from your local bookshop and are also available by post from:

**Bookpost, PO Box 29, Douglas, Isle of Man IM99 1BQ**

Credit cards accepted. For details:
Telephone: 01624 677237
Fax: 01624 670923
Email: bookshop@enterprise.net
www.bookpost.co.uk

**Free postage and packing in the United Kingdom**